Papa's Panda

Papa's Panda

By Nancy Willard
Illustrated by
Lillian Hoban

Harcourt Brace Jovanovich   New York and London

Printed in the United States of America

LIBRARY OF CONGRESS CATALOGING IN PUBLICATION DATA
Willard, Nancy.
Papa's Panda
SUMMARY: Papa's yarn about a giant panda
makes James long for one of his own.
[1. Pandas—Fiction]   I. Hoban, Lillian.
II. Title.
PZ7.W6553Pap   [E]   78–31787
ISBN 0-15-332875-4   (Library: 10 different titles)
ISBN 0-15-332892-4   (Single title, 4 copies)
ISBN 0-15-332952-1   (Replacement single copy)

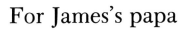

For James's papa

That morning Papa came instead of
Mama to wake up James, and Papa sang
to him, "Happy birthday to you! Happy
birthday to you!"

"Where's my present?" demanded
James.

"Mama's wrapping it," said Papa.

"Is it a teddy?" asked James. "I really want a teddy bear like Danny Jackson's."

"What kind of teddy does Danny Jackson have?"

"It's brown and eats crackers," said James.

"I don't think Mama is wrapping a brown teddy that eats crackers," said Papa.

"But I want a teddy like Danny's."

"You haven't even seen your present yet," said Papa.

"I don't want to see it!" shouted James. "I won't open it!"

"Then I'll open it for you," said Papa.

"Then I'll throw it away," said James. "I want a teddy like Danny's."

"I don't know why you want a teddy that looks like somebody else's. I never even wanted a teddy when I was a boy. I wanted a panda."

"A real panda?" asked James.

"No, a toy panda. The real pandas live in China."

"Can we ever get a real panda for a pet?" asked James.

Papa shook his head. "There are not many real pandas left. If there is a keeper of pandas in China, I am sure he would not let us keep one for a pet."

"But maybe the keeper of pandas would let a panda visit us," said James.

"Oh, visit!" exclaimed Papa. "That's quite another thing. If a panda wished to visit us, the keeper might let him."

"How could he come?" asked James.
"By airplane?"

"By airplane," said Papa. "He would
come by airplane."

"And he would order some ginger
ale—" said James.

"No, he wouldn't," said Papa. "Pandas like bamboo. He would order juice of bamboo on ice."

"And after the juice of bamboo on ice?" asked James.

"He would drink juice of bamboo on
ice until the plane landed in New York,"
said Papa. "And we would be there to
meet him."

"Suppose we couldn't find him," said
James.

"Oh, but we could," said Papa. "Pandas are big."

"How big?"

"As big as I am," said Papa.

"Suppose he doesn't fit in the car?" asked James.

"We would have to buy a bus," said Papa.

"But suppose we don't have enough money to buy a bus?" asked James.

"Why, we would all go to work. Mama would work, you would work."

"What would I work at?" asked James.
"You would run the elevator at
Wallace's.

"And after work we would eat our supper and go directly to bed because we'd be so tired."

"And the panda—where would he sleep?" asked James.

"With you," said Papa. "He's your panda."

"But my bed is too small!" said James.

"Then Mama and you and I would push our beds together for him," suggested Papa.

"And where would we sleep?" asked James.

"On the floor," said Papa.

"Why can't the panda sleep on the floor?"

"Why," said Papa, "because he's the guest.

"And since he's coming from the
bamboo forest, he won't have any clothes.
I would have to give him my new suit."

"Do pandas wear clothes?" asked James.

Papa shook his head.

"Not in the forest. But this panda would see my new suit, which I would be wearing when I met him at the airport. And he would say, 'I WANT A SUIT. I WANT A SUIT JUST LIKE YOURS.'"

"Would it fit him?" asked James.

"No. He'd burst all the seams. This panda is very fat—"

"—because he eats a lot," said James. "And he's always hungry."

"Oh, very hungry," said Papa. "First he'd ask for bamboo leaves and we wouldn't have any.

"Then he'd say, 'WHAT ELSE HAVE YOU GOT FOR A PANDA TO EAT?'"

"And then he'd open the refrigerator
and eat up all the ice cream.

"And then he'd take a bottle of milk to drink in the living room, and he'd spill it on the sofa. And you would spank him," said James.

"No, I wouldn't," said Papa. "He's too big. He'd say, 'GET OFF MY SOFA!' And maybe he'd spank me."

"And would you cry?" asked James.

"I might cry," said Papa, "if he spanks me very hard."

"Don't worry, Papa. Maybe he won't come."

"Maybe he won't come till winter, anyway," said Papa. "That will give us all time to learn Chinese."

"Why do we have to learn Chinese?"

"So we can talk to the panda."

"Is Chinese hard to learn?"

"For me, yes," said Papa. "I am sure it will be hard for me."

"We'll have to learn it fast," said James, "because he might be on his way right now. And he'll march up to the front door and knock three times—"

"And Mama and I will hide under the bed," said Papa, "and you will answer the door."

"Why do I have to answer the door?"

"Because this panda listens to children but not to grownups. So when you open the door, you must say to him very gently, 'I am sorry but I already have a panda.'"

"But I don't have a panda," exclaimed James. "I DON'T HAVE A PANDA!"

At that moment Mama put her head in the door of James's room.

"What's all the yelling about?" she asked.

"I need a panda," said James. "I need one right away."

"It just so happens," said Mama, "that you have a panda."

And she handed James a box wrapped in red paper. He tore off the paper and lifted the lid of the box. There lay a panda. A little one.